B55 012 416 4

KT-546-733

Tales from Mossy Bottom Farm

PRANKS
A LOT!

D

'17

- 5

2 5 A

0 2
11 A

- 1

This b

The lo
a furth

This is a work of fiction. Names, characters, places and incidents are either the product of the author's imagination or, if real, are used fictitiously. All statements, activities, stunts, descriptions, information and material of any kind contained herein are included for entertainment purposes only and should not be relied on for accuracy or replicated as they may result in injury.

First published 2016 by Walker Entertainment, an imprint of Walker Books Ltd, 87 Vauxhall Walk, London SE11 5HJ

2 4 6 8 10 9 7 5 3 1

Written by Martin Howard and illustrated by Andy Janes
© and TM Aardman Animations Limited 2016. All rights reserved. Shaun the Sheep (word mark) and the character Shaun the Sheep are trademarks used under licence from Aardman Animations Limited.

This book has been typeset in Manticore

Printed and bound in Great Britain by Clays Ltd, St Ives plc

All rights reserved. No part of this book may be reproduced, transmitted, or stored in an information retrieval system in any form or by any means, graphic, electronic or mechanical, including photocopying, taping and recording, without prior written permission from the publisher.

British Library Cataloguing in Publication Data:
a catalogue record for this book is available from the British Library

ISBN 978-1-4063-6622-8

www.walker.co.uk

Rotherham Libraries	
B55 012 416 4	
PETERS	29-Jun-2016
	£4.99

Tales from Mossy Bottom Farm

PRANKS A LOT!

Martin Howard

Illustrated by Andy Janes

WALKER
ENTERTAINMENT

SHAUN is the leader of the Flock. He's clever, cool and always keeps his head when the other sheep are losing theirs.

BITZER

The Farmer's faithful dog and a good friend to Shaun, Bitzer's the ever suffering sheepdog doing his best to keep Shaun's pals out of trouble.

THE FARMER

Running the farm with Bitzer at his side, the Farmer is completely unaware of the Flock's human-like intelligence ... and their shenanigans.

THE FLOCK

One big happy (if slightly dopey) family, the sheep like to play and create mischief together, though it's usually Shaun and Bitzer who sort out the resulting mess.

TIMMY

He may be the baby of the Flock, but Timmy is often at the centre of things. It's a good job his mum is always there to keep him safe.

TIMMY'S MUM

The very loving – if sometimes absent-minded – mother of Timmy, she is recognizable by the curlers in her fleece.

THE OWL

A bit of a night owl, this observant bird is usually found in the barnyard tree. He is known for being wise – or at least wisecracking.

CONTENTS

CHAPTER ONE:

DRAWN INTO A PRANK

Dust danced in the film projector's beam of light. Sitting on rows of hay bales in the dark barn, the Flock munched popcorn and gazed up at the evening's film, an educational movie called *How to Grow a Prize-Winning Turnip*. A few years ago, the Farmer had bought the film because he dreamed of winning the gold cup at the Mossy Bottom Turnip Festival – a dream that had died when he presented the turnip that he had raised all summer with love and care. It was exactly the same shape as a very small bottom. Instead of winning the cup, the Farmer had been awarded a plastic mug bearing the words **"WORLD'S STUPIDEST TURNIP"**.

In disgust, he had tossed the movie, the mug and the turnip into the back of the shed and sworn that he was finished with root vegetables for ever.

Shaun grinned as he remembered that the Farmer had started planting radishes just a week later, vowing that they would be the biggest radishes ever grown. When it came to root vegetables, the Farmer just couldn't stop.

Balancing on the edge of his hay bale, Shaun watched the film. It wasn't very exciting. In his opinion there weren't quite enough car chases and explosions and big dance scenes. Only Nuts was really enjoying it. From the corner of his eye, Shaun saw him wipe away tears when the star pulled a huge turnip from the ground and showed it proudly to the camera.

Now the movie was coming up to the big finish. The star was washing the muck off his turnip and was about to lay it next to some smaller turnips, which hadn't been grown using his amazing methods. Shaun sat forward. It wasn't a great movie, but he'd sat through an hour of turnips and he wasn't going to miss the ending.

Bitzer slumped against him, snoring in his ear. Shaun was almost deafened by the sound, which was not unlike the noise of someone slurping the last of a milkshake through a straw. Glaring, Shaun shoved the sheepdog away.

Bitzer mumbled and tried to sit up, then fell back onto Shaun's shoulder. It had been a long day, ticking things off on his clipboard, blowing his whistle and leaning against the gate. He was dog-tired.

Making happy "mmmmfmmmm" noises, he wriggled around to get comfy and started snoring again.

A dribble of drool leaked from the corner of his mouth and soaked into Shaun's fleece.

Ugh. Wrinkling his nose, Shaun scowled at the sheepdog, then looked up at the sound of Nuts stamping his hooves, whooping and clapping. The credits were rolling.

He had missed the end of the movie, and it was all Bitzer's fault!

Furious, he pushed the dog away again. This time, Bitzer fell back on the hay bale, still snoring.

Bitzer had ruined the movie. Some sort of punishment was in order. Peering around the dim barn, Shaun spotted a bucket of cold water. *Pouring it over Bitzer's head might be fun,* he thought. But that didn't seem hilarious enough.

He noticed a ball of hairy string that had rolled into a corner. Shaun stroked his chin. What if he tied Bitzer's feet together and *then* dumped a bucket of cold water on his head? Then, when Bitzer jumped up and tried to chase him...

Shaun looked around the barn for more ideas, and then paused. A cheeky grin broke out on his face. Hanging by the door was Bitzer's clipboard, and next to it was a black felt-tip pen.

Shaun had just thought of something even funnier.

It was brilliant. Bitzer looked ridiculous.

Timmy was the first to laugh, pressing a tiny hoof against his mouth to avoid waking the sheepdog. His laughter was infectious. Shoulders heaving, Hazel clamped a hoof to her mouth too. The Twins snickered, then bleated loud guffaws. Within seconds the whole barn was shaking to the sound of sheep laughter.

Bitzer's eyes flickered open. Confused, he sat up and looked around. What was going on? He didn't have a clue why everyone was cracking up, which made it even funnier for the Flock, setting them off into fresh peals of laughter. Teeth clamped together, Shirley made "mmmfff mmmmfff" sounds. Nuts plunged his head into the bucket of water. Bubbles rose to the surface, each one letting off a giggling sound as it popped.

Struggling to maintain a straight face, Shaun simply shrugged at the sheepdog. He had no idea what the Flock thought was so funny.

Sheep! Spinning a paw by his ear to say that they were all bonkers, Bitzer stamped off. With a CRASH, the barn door slammed behind him. Whuffing darkly under his breath, he made his way home to bed, sheep laughter still ringing in his ears.

In the moonlight, an owl blinked down from a tree as Bitzer passed, then hooted with laughter.

CHAPTER TWO:

A FACE FULL OF COWPAT

Pong!

The next morning, Bitzer scratched his head in the middle of the yard. The whole farm seemed to have gone completely mad.

Everywhere he went, he was followed by squeals and clucks and quacks and bleats of laughter. What was so funny? When they saw him coming, the pigs stared, then rolled in the muck, pointing at him and snorting with glee. The rooster laughed so hard he fell off

23

the gatepost. Soon all the hens were flapping about the chicken run. Mowermouth the goat had actually stopped eating for a few seconds, a half-munched cabbage dropping from his mouth as Bitzer passed by.

Even the ducks whispered behind their wings and tittered to one another. Before Bitzer's bewildered eyes, they began parading up and down the farmyard with pondweed draped across their beaks like moustaches.

The flock was all lined up at the meadow wall, their eyes following Bitzer round the farm. Every time he glanced back at them they lowered their heads to hide their grins.

Bitzer frowned. Why was everyone laughing at him?

He checked his rear end. He hadn't sat in wet paint. He took his hat off and looked at it. It was the same old hat. He hadn't put a pair of the Farmer's underpants on his head by mistake ... again.

Perhaps, he thought to himself, the animals weren't laughing at him. Perhaps he was just missing the joke. Bitzer pretended to laugh along with them, chuckling nervously as he looked around at the staring animals.

Waves of fresh laughter rolled across Mossy Bottom Farm. Bitzer watched in dismay as Shaun lay in the grass, clutching his tummy and kicking his legs in the air, tears rolling down his face.

Shaking his head, Bitzer turned his back on them. The farm had gone crazy, but he – Bitzer – would maintain his dignity. Ignoring the laughter, he walked stiffly across the yard and checked his clipboard. The Farmer's wellington boots needed a polish before breakfast, but, glancing up at the bedroom window, he saw that the Farmer was still in his pyjamas. Bitzer had just enough time for a cuppa.

A few minutes later, sipping his tea by the kennel, Bitzer blinked at the dim reflection in his mug. Something wasn't quite right. He checked his face in the water bowl.

Bitzer's jaw dropped in horror. The silly spectacles, the ridiculous moustache... The reason for the animals' glee became crystal clear. They *had* been laughing at him all along.

Shaun!

This was *Shaun's* handiwork. A grim look settled on Bitzer's face. A growl rumbled at the back of his throat. Shaun would *pay*. Already, a plan was coming together. He dipped his hat into the water bowl and dabbed at the ink on his face, deep in thought.

Oh yes, he – Bitzer – was not the sort of dog to let something like this pass. He would strike back, and sooner – *much* sooner – than Shaun expected. With a glance up at the bedroom window to make sure the Farmer was still dressing, he jogged over to the kitchen door. There was just one little thing he needed to borrow...

Half an hour later, Bitzer stood in the lane and turned his **STOP** sign to **GO**. The Flock began to cross. Even though Bitzer had washed away the pen marks on his face, the sheep still giggled and grinned up at him as they passed. Bitzer pretended not to notice. *Soon,* he told himself. Soon he would have his revenge. His face wore a cheerful, nothing-to-see-here smile, but inside he was cackling with wicked glee.

While the Farmer closed the gate behind him, Bitzer ran ahead of the Flock, peeping on his whistle and holding out an arm to point the way to the food troughs. The hungry sheep shoved and jostled to be first in the queue.

Bitzer's whistle peeped again: a sheep down, a sheep *down*!

Shaun lifted his face, blinking through a thick mask of brown muck. Wiping the sludge from his eyes, he sniffed at the brown mess on his hoof and groaned. He had tripped straight into a huge cowpat! Above him, the Farmer took a step back, his face screwed up in disgust. "Huuummphwarg," he rumbled, holding his nose. He pointed at Bitzer, then jerked his thumb back towards the farm.

Bitzer nodded, chuckling silently to himself. Stage One of his revenge was complete, and everything was going exactly as planned. With a quiet heh, heh, heh, he peeped his whistle once more and held out a paw towards the sheep dip.

Bath time.

CHAPTER THREE:

DYE, SHAUN, DYE!

Peeep, peep, peep, peep. Bitzer's whistle blasting in his ear, Shaun scowled through his cowpat face mask. Bleats of laughter rolled across Mossy Bottom Farm once again. Bitzer had got his own back with style!

Gritting his teeth as he was frogmarched back across the lane, Shaun sighed and gave the sheepdog a grin. Bitzer had only returned the prank. It was only fair, even if Shaun did smell of cowpat now. Shivering on the edge of the dip, he watched the sheepdog turn on the taps and pour in half a packet of **BARRY STILES' SPARKLE CLEAN SHEEP DIP**. As it foamed, Bitzer returned his smile, pointed at the shed and whuffed. He would fetch Shaun a towel and a rubber duck to play with.

Watching the sheepdog disappear round the side of the barn, Shaun had a warm and fuzzy feeling inside. Even after the pranks, Bitzer was so kind.

Shaun jumped into the pool. As he came up for air, he decided that he would never, ever prank the sheepdog again.

The sheep dip was perfect. Shaun rolled onto his back and floated in the foam with his eyes closed. Hearing a small splash, he half-opened his eyes and saw Bitzer with one paw in the water, making sure the temperature was just right. *What a dog*, Shaun thought.

As Shaun's eyes closed again, Bitzer grinned to himself.

Shaun opened his eyes half an hour later and saw Bitzer standing on the side of the sheep dip, holding up a towel. With a sigh, Shaun climbed out of the pool, took the towel and frowned. Something was wrong with Bitzer's face. It was all screwed up. And why was he making snorting, choking noises?

Shaun bleated. Was Bitzer feeling all right?

In response, Bitzer collapsed. Tears rolled down his face. Clutching his stomach with one paw, he pointed at Shaun with the other.

Shaun glared. There was nothing funny about a sheep getting out of the bath. Grumpily, he began drying himself, glancing down to check that every last speck of cowpat was gone. His fleece was pink. Otherwise everything was fine...

Pink?

Shaun blinked, and looked again.

Pink!

His wool had turned bright, glaring, bubblegum pink.

Startled, he glanced back at Bitzer, who was still howling with laughter. Now, though, he was holding up an empty bottle of red food colouring.

Shaun stared at the bottle, and then down at his fleece. His jaw fell open. He had been pranked! Again! The cowpat hadn't been enough revenge for Bitzer. He had made Shaun look like a fairground candyfloss too!

His moment of horror was interrupted by a squeaking noise. Spinning round, Shaun saw Timmy pointing and bouncing up and down with glee. The little sheep was joined by Hazel. Standing by the edge of the pool, she giggled and waved to the other sheep. They had to see this.

Suddenly, Bitzer stopped laughing and scrambled to his feet. Behind the approaching sheep, the Farmer was closing the gate. In his haste to prank Shaun, Bitzer had forgotten all about the Farmer! If the Farmer saw a bright pink Shaun, there would be big trouble.

Flapping his arms in a panic, Bitzer dashed across the yard.

With a click, the gate closed. Humming his favourite pop tune – **"TURNIP THE FUNKY BEET"** – the Farmer started ambling towards the farmhouse. The animals were fed, so he could put his feet up for a few moments with the newspaper and a mug of tea.

Then he saw Bitzer bounding towards him, tongue hanging out and arms waving madly. The Farmer chuckled to himself. He'd only been away for ten minutes, but silly, loyal Bitzer had obviously missed him. "Gooby," he mumbled. "Eeesagoobyinny…"

CRASH.

Bitzer hit him like a cannonball. "Oooofwarraflippineck…" Arms full of dog, the Farmer staggered and fell backwards into the gate. In the tussle, his glasses flew off. Cursing, he shoved the sheepdog away and groped around on the ground.

Meanwhile, oinks, clucks and bleats drifted across the farmyard. There was a commotion by the sheep dip. Staggering to his feet, the Farmer blinked and squinted. The sheep and chickens had crowded round something outside the pigs' enclosure, and they were making a lot of noise.

The Farmer squinted again. What on earth were they making such a fuss about? Without his glasses, he could just make out a pink blob. *Pink!* He gasped. A pig! A pig had escaped!

Half-blind, the Farmer growled at Bitzer to stay, then stumbled across the farmyard, shouting.

At the centre of the crowd of animals, Shaun didn't see the Farmer until it was too late. "Ooogotcha," muttered the Farmer, pushing sheep aside and catching him under one arm.

Shaun struggled, bleating, but the Farmer ignored him. With a satisfied grunt, he heaved him over the wall.

Sperrr-latt.

As the Farmer walked away, wiping his hands, Shaun looked up from a deep pool of muck. A pig squealed and keeled over in a giggling fit, sending up a wave of fresh mud that rained down over Shaun.

A line of sheep's faces appeared over the wall, every single one of them bleating with laughter. At the end of the line, Bitzer waved the Farmer's glasses, smirked and gave the pink, filthy sheep a wink. He had been well and truly pranked – Bitzer style.

CHAPTER FOUR:

JAMMING

The barn door creaked open a few centimetres. Shaun peered through the crack at the silver, moonlit farm. All was quiet. The only sounds were the distant grunts of sleeping pigs and the drowsy bu-kiiiirk of chickens. Clutching a jar, Shaun tiptoed across the yard, his shadow huge on the side of the barn. He ignored the owl snickering at him on a branch above.

If Bitzer wanted to play dirty, then Shaun could play dirty too.

Moving like a ninja, Shaun pressed his ear to the side of Bitzer's kennel. He could hear the dog chuckling in his sleep. Shaun scowled. Slowly, slowly, he reached through the open doorway, his tongue between his teeth as he felt his way around. He patted something soft and guessed it to be Bitzer's head.

The sheepdog whuffed happily. Pats on the head meant he was a Good Boy. Still fast asleep, he rolled onto his back for a tummy tickle.

Shaun's hoof moved on, patting a bone, a mug, something that felt like a snooker table, a drum kit, a grandfather clock and another bone, until he found what he was looking for. He withdrew his arm carefully, clutching his find, and grinned in the moonlight. *Success!* Carefully, he tipped the contents of his jar into Bitzer's hat, returned the hat to its place inside the kennel and crept back to bed.

Bitzer woke to the sound of the cockerel crowing. He yawned. Another day on Mossy Bottom Farm.

Still half asleep, he pulled on his hat. Then he frowned. Something didn't feel quite right, but his sleepy brain was foggy and he couldn't work out what it was. With a shrug he tucked a roll of toilet paper and a copy of **THE MOSSY BOTTOM GAZETTE** under his arm and set off for his favourite tree.

Sitting happily, he opened the newspaper. A Mossy Bottom man had opened a new paper shop, he read. But it had folded after a few weeks. Also, a lorry loaded with tortoises had crashed into a lamppost. The reporter called it a turtle disaster.

Bitzer shook his head, sadly. What was the world coming to? He heard a faint droning sound in the distance. Turning the page, he

saw that the corner shop was having a sale ...
on corners. He scratched his head. As he did
so, a squelching noise came from his hat.

Puzzled, Bitzer scratched his head again.

A red blob trickled down his face and
plopped onto the open newspaper. Bitzer
stared at it in shock. He was *bleeding*.

Bitzer's heart thumped. He felt woozy. He needed an ambulance...

Then his nose twitched at the scent. Gingerly, he dabbed the blob with his paw and tasted it. Bitzer's eyes widened. The red blob wasn't blood: it was raspberry jam. He wasn't bleeding: he was raspberry jamming! There was raspberry jam in his hat. How had it got there?

Bitzer stared as another blob dripped onto his paper, and then he jumped up with a start. He would solve the mystery later. Right now, he had to get to a slice of toast before all the jam leaked away.

The droning sound was louder now.

Bubbles of air rose to the surface. The wasps buzzed above for a moment or two, but they quickly gave up and swarmed back towards the Farmer's breakfast.

Bitzer's head emerged from the pond, like a monster rising from the deep. Covered in slime, he spat out a fountain of water. Perched on top of his head was a lily pad, upon which sat a confused frog. Peering down, the frog stamped on Bitzer's head with a webbed foot and hopped back into the water with a plop.

Laughter rang out all across Mossy Bottom Farm.

Wiping pond scum from his eyes, Bitzer growled. He and Shaun had been even, but Shaun had gone ahead and pranked him again.

This meant war.

BITZER 1-0 SHAUN

CHAPTER FIVE:

THE UN-FUNNY BONE

Prank followed prank as long summer day followed long summer day. In retaliation for the jam, Bitzer burst a blown-up paper bag behind the Farmer while he was shearing Shaun. Almost jumping out of his skin, the Farmer shaved a wiggly line of baldness into Shaun's fleece.

Shaun pranked the sheepdog right back by slipping a mousetrap into his tea mug.

BITZER 1–1 SHAUN

But, slowly, the laughter dried up. The Flock watched in wonder, then bewilderment, then worry. The pranks were getting out of hand. Someone was going to get seriously hurt.

In revenge for the mousetrap, Bitzer poured pepper into Shaun's bed. The next morning Shaun awoke with a terrible case of the itches, certain he had fleas. Keeping a careful eye on Bitzer, he had found a bottle of **FLEEZAWAY** in the shed. But when the Flock had hosed him down, Shaun realized that Bitzer had poured away the anti-flea medicine and replaced it with **EXTRA VOLUME AND BOUNCE** shampoo. Shaun's fleece swelled up like a balloon, and for the rest of the day he waddled round the farm looking like a cross between a cloud and a poodle.

BITZER 2-1 SHAUN

Under cover of darkness, Shaun tied Bitzer's kennel to the tractor's towbar. Bitzer didn't notice the rope until his home shot past him at high speed during his morning rounds. Horrified, the sheepdog dropped his clipboard and tried to stop the runaway kennel by throwing himself on top of it. For the next twenty minutes, the animals stared as the sheepdog rode his kennel like a rodeo bull-rider as it bounced and jolted up and down the field behind the tractor.

Bitzer and Shaun became shifty. Both spent their days eyeing each other, constantly on the lookout for the next prank. Shaun chalked complicated drawings on the blackboard. Bitzer neglected his work, scribbling plan after plan on his clipboard. If their paths crossed, the sheep and sheepdog walked on by with noses in the air. Then, as soon as they were out of each other's sight, they returned to plotting.

Shaun spent a secretive day in the barn making a fake, hollow bone with wet paper, paste and white paint. When it dried, he filled it with rabbit droppings and left it outside Bitzer's kennel. Sniggering, he watched as the sheepdog chewed into it and subsequently spent three hours trying to scrape rabbit poo off his tongue.

The next morning, Shaun found a large present waiting outside the barn, with a note from Bitzer saying he was sorry for all the pranks. A tear in his eye, Shaun reached for the giant bow on top—and bleated in terror when a huge gorilla leapt out at him, baring its teeth and beating its chest in fury. The gorilla chased him twice round the farm, past staring animals, until Shaun scampered up a tree.

Hearing hoots of laughter below, Shaun glared down and saw Bitzer shaking off the head of the Farmer's Halloween gorilla costume and collapsing onto the grass, clutching his stomach.

Shaking
his head
sadly, Shaun
clung to a branch
and gazed around
at the farm. None
of the other animals
even watched the pranks
any more. By the hen house,
the chickens were more entertained
scratching in the dirt. Timmy was using
Hazel's kite as a hang-glider. Even the pigs
didn't bother to look, sunbathing happily in
the pools of mud that kept their skin looking
young and reduced the fine lines of ageing.

Shaun sighed to himself, remembering
his relief when he had read the apologetic
note on Bitzer's "present". The pranks were
out of control. They weren't fun any more.

Worse: they were ruining his friendship with Bitzer. With a sorrowful bleat, Shaun climbed down from the tree.

Growling, Bitzer scrambled to his feet and backed away. He didn't know what trickery Shaun was planning next, but he figured he'd better keep his distance. Shaun sat in the grass, put his head in his hooves and bleated. He was tired of pranks. Pointing to the other animals enjoying themselves, he bleated again. Didn't Bitzer think it was time to stop too?

Bitzer blinked at him suspiciously, then whuffed. Stop the pranks?

Shaun nodded.

Slowly, the sheepdog nodded. Did that mean he had won?

Shaun shrugged. He didn't care. Turning his back on Bitzer, he trotted away to join the hang-gliding fun.

Sweating in the gorilla costume, Bitzer watched him go. His eyes narrowed. Did Shaun think he was completely stupid? Pretending to stop the pranks, Bitzer was certain, was all part of Shaun's next prank.

CHAPTER SIX:

SPOT THE PLOT

The days that followed were full of sunshine, and giggles, and kite hang-gliding, and wheelbarrow races, and sheep jousting, and lazing around in the meadow. The only thing that worried Shaun was Bitzer. The sheepdog had started acting more strangely than ever. Every time Shaun turned round, he caught Bitzer peering at him. Bitzer would immediately duck below a wall or look away quickly, shading his eyes, whistling and gazing up at clouds floating past.

On one occasion, Shaun had caught him hiding under an old tin bath in the barn. Bitzer gurgled in embarrassment when Shaun lifted it, and patted the ground as if he had just finished burying a bone.

Meanwhile, as the days passed, Bitzer became more and more convinced that Shaun was sneakily planning something *big*... Well, it seemed Shaun had forgotten that sheepdogs were brimming with intelligence and cunning. Whenever Shaun decided to launch his prank, he – Bitzer – would be ready. In the meantime, he was keeping a very beady eye on Shaun.

Late one night, Bitzer crept into the barn and tiptoed past the sleeping sheep to check out the blackboard, which had been covered in a sheet. He lifted the fabric.

The black surface of the board had been wiped clean of chalk; there wasn't a mark on it.

Mighty suspicious, Bitzer growled softly to himself. Clearly, this was proof that Shaun was carefully covering his tracks.

The next day, Bitzer peeped round the corner of the farmhouse and saw Shaun rummaging in the shed. What was he looking for? Bitzer ducked back as Shaun emerged and trotted back towards the meadow, dragging a hose. Narrowing his eyes, Bitzer nodded to himself. As Bitzer had suspected all along, Shaun was secretly building some kind of water-spraying prank contraption.

Bitzer's suspicions were confirmed the next morning as the sheep filed across the lane to their breakfast. Shaun's turn came to walk past Bitzer, and he looked up and gave the sheepdog a big smile and a wink.

Bitzer stared, gurgling to himself in disbelief. Shaun was so sure that Bitzer was clueless about his dirty, underhand prank plans that he was openly *smiling* at him. And *winking* too. Of all the barefaced, brazen

cheek! Bitzer ground his teeth together. Shaun might think Bitzer was a fool, but he'd soon learn not to mess with Bitzer ... the hard way. Bitzer would prank Shaun before Shaun had a chance to prank him.

Chuckling the famous chuckle of a sheepdog hatching a plot, Bitzer closed the gate carefully. The sheep would be busy for a while. He had plenty of time to fetch the Farmer's shovel from the shed and prepare a surprise that Shaun would never forget.

CHAPTER SEVEN:

LAUGH TILL IT HURTS

Moonlight shone through holes in the roof and pooled on the floor, giving the barn a soft glow. Shaun brushed his teeth, then spat into a bucket, smiling to himself.

It had been another classic summer day on Mossy Bottom Farm. A city family had spread their picnic in one corner of the meadow, before the sight of Shirley rumbling towards them like a speeding tank had sent them screaming. Shaun could still taste the cake. Afterwards, the Flock had played Water Pistol Cowboy and a new game Shaun had invented, called Flicking Cowpats at the Pigs.

Shaun yawned. It had been a grand day, and now he was looking forward to tomorrow. He had plans for a cowpat-flicking machine that would double the fun. He trotted over to his bed, closed his eyes, put his hooves behind his head and let himself fall back into the soft pile of straw.

KERR-ASSSSSHHH!

With a terrified bleat, Shaun fell straight *through* his bed and into a deep hole beneath.

SPLOSH!

At the bottom was a tin bath, now only half-full of cold water and pond slime.

Spitting out a stream of dirty water, Shaun surfaced, blinking. Above him, silhouetted in the moonlight, a darkened figure danced about in glee, howling with laughter and pointing down at him.

Shaun scowled.

Bitzer.

Bitzer had broken the truce.

The sheepdog moonwalked round the top of the hole and punched the air, whuffing.

He was the *winner*. Shaun had been pranked yet again!

In reply, Shaun let out a pathetic and painful bleat. Bitzer ignored him, jigging about in triumph.

More faces appeared at the top of the hole. Hazel, the Twins, Nuts, Timmy's Mum in her age-defying night-time face mask, Shirley... Soon the whole Flock was crowded round, peering down at Shaun.

A loud bleat interrupted Bitzer's victory moonwalk. Stumbling to a halt, he looked up to see a row of angry faces. Timmy's Mum bleated again. She jabbed a hoof into his chest and then pointed down the hole.

Bitzer's laughter trailed off. Following the pointing hoof with his eyes, he saw Shaun splashing about, trying to climb out of the bath. With a defeated bleat, Shaun sank back into the smelly water, clutching his leg.

Bitzer looked around. The sheep glared back at him. Shirley crossed her arms and tapped a hoof in disgust. Hazel tutted, shaking her head. Noses in the air, the Twins turned their backs on the sheepdog. Nuts stared down the hole in wonder. He would *never* have guessed that the barn had a secret indoor swimming pool!

Once again, Shaun bleated in pain.

The realization that Shaun was hurt filled Bitzer with horror. Whuffing, he pointed sheep to every corner of the barn. He was going to need ropes, and a ladder, and safety equipment. Whatever the danger, he was going into the hole himself, and he wasn't coming out without Shaun!

A few minutes later, after lifting a sopping Shaun up to the barn floor, Bitzer snapped on a surgical mask made from a handkerchief and a length of hairy string. He held out a paw. Hazel passed him a large, rusty saw.

Sitting up, Shaun bleated in terror.

Bitzer looked at the saw, rolled his eyes, and then gave Hazel an annoyed whuff. He put the saw down in a safe spot on the floor and instead got to work with soapy water, sticks and a torn-up sheet.

Before long, Shaun was spotlessly clean. With his bandaged leg looking like an enormous white sausage, he lay back in a soft bed that Bitzer had arranged, propped up on comfy pillows. By Shaun's side stood an old tin can filled with daisies and dandelions. Bitzer had been unable to find grapes, but he had pulled a bunch of funny-looking radishes from the Farmer's vegetable garden instead.

Alongside them was a get-well-soon card that the sheepdog had hurriedly drawn with crayons. On the front was a picture of Bitzer with a tear in his eye and his arm around Shaun. Underneath, Bitzer had written **BEST FRIENDS FOREVER.**

Closing his eyes, Shaun let out a small snore and snuggled further down while Bitzer tucked him in and tiptoed away. As the barn door squeaked closed behind him, Shaun opened his eyes.

Putting a hoof to his lips, he gave the watching Flock a huge wink.

CHAPTER EIGHT:

SICKBED SHAUN

Later, Bitzer came to visit his injured friend. With a groan, Shaun lay back on his pillows and turned his head to one side. He didn't want Bitzer to see him in such pain. At his bedside, the sheepdog hopped from one paw to another in agonies of guilt. He whuffed, mournfully. Was there anything – *anything* – he could fetch that might make Shaun feel better?

The corners of Shaun's mouth twitched.

Hiding the smile under another groan, he looked around at the empty plates, cups and glasses that surrounded his bed. He bleated. Bitzer had already been *sooooo* kind; he couldn't possibly ask for anything else.

Bitzer's tail wagged. He panted eagerly. Whatever Shaun wanted, Bitzer would go and fetch it.

Giving in, Shaun grabbed Bitzer's clipboard and started scribbling.

Bitzer's eyes widened as Shaun turned the page and tapped it. The list continued overleaf. Bitzer whuffed nervously. This was a lot...

Squeezing his eyes closed in pain, Shaun bleated weakly, waving a hoof towards the door. He understood. Bitzer was a busy dog with much better things to do than look after him. Shaun would be fine. In fact, he should probably get up. With an enormous effort, he tried to stand ... before flopping back against the pillows with a fresh bleat of pain.

Bitzer yelped, pushing Shaun back into bed and fussing with the blankets until he was comfortably tucked in again. Wagging a stern paw, he gestured for Shaun to stay in bed. Bitzer would find some way to bring him everything on the list. Peering down at Shaun's list, he muttered to himself. He would have to break open his piggy bank...

As the sheepdog walked away, scratching his head, Shaun snickered to himself and settled back against his soft pillows with a copy of **SHEEP GOSSIP** magazine. Being hurt was shaping up to be even more fun than flicking cow plop at the pigs.

By bedtime, Shaun could hardly be seen behind a pile of empty pizza boxes, ice-cream tubs, sweet wrappers and popcorn buckets.

Happy burps echoed round the barn as Bitzer put away the projector and screen. *How to Grow a Prize-Winning Turnip* still wasn't a great movie, but at least this time Bitzer hadn't drooled and snored through the ending. Remembering to give a little whimper of pain, Shaun pulled the covers up under his chin. He was feeling sleepy now. Pointing towards the door, he waggled a hoof. Bitzer should go to bed too...

Bitzer nodded, wiping his forehead with one paw. Nursing Shaun all day had been tiring, and he still had his evening rounds to do.

With a bleat, Shaun passed him an empty mug. Before Bitzer went to bed, Shaun could use another mug of hot chocolate.

Half an hour later, a weary Bitzer dragged his feet round the farm, counting off chickens and checking gates and jealously glancing up at the bedroom window where the Farmer was tucking his teddy into bed.

It was his own fault, Bitzer told himself. If he hadn't been so suspicious, he wouldn't have played the stupid prank. Guilt gnawed at him. *Poor Shaun,* he thought. *His leg looked so painful. Bitzer was a Bad Dog...*

Above his head, an owl hooted in the moonlight and held its wing up so the feathers looked like a moustache. Bitzer glared.

Faint sounds of laughter drifted across the meadow from the barn. Bitzer raised an ear. What was going on now? Creeping across the grass, he sneaked up the side of the barn and held an eye to a knothole in the wall.

For almost a minute he stared at the scene, disbelieving. Then a low growl rumbled in the back of his throat.

Inside the barn, the sheep were queuing up to limbo dance under a stick held by the Twins. As Bitzer watched, Shaun's turn came. Laughing with glee, and loose bandages trailing from his leg, he leaned backwards and shimmied beneath the stick, then jumped round the barn raising up his hooves in triumph.

There was nothing wrong with him at all.

Shaun had done it again: Bitzer had been pranked!

CHAPTER NINE:

ROOM SERVICE

In the farmhouse, the Farmer blinked in confusion at his I ♥ **MUCKSPREADERS** calendar. Underneath the picture of a pretty girl posing on a heap of manure was a scrawled note: he had a dentist's appointment! He scratched his head, certain that he had seen the dentist the week before. He remembered it clearly because the dentist had knelt on his chest, sweating with effort as he drilled out a tooth.

It had been quite uncomfortable. *Even so*, he grumbled to himself, *an appointment was an appointment*, and if he didn't hurry he'd be late.

From behind a bush, Bitzer watched the Farmer's car judder into life and disappear down the lane. Humming, Bitzer took the handles of a wheelbarrow and rolled it towards the barn.

The door creaked open, spilling sunshine into the barn. Shaun quickly wiped the grin off his face and lay back on his pillows with a painful groan. He smiled weakly and struggled to sit, bleating pathetically. Could Bitzer possibly fetch him a small glass of water ... and a breakfast pizza, and some new magazines, and some grapes, and some more ice cream? Ice cream was definitely helping his leg feel better.

Bitzer patted Shaun's hoof. With a quiet whuff, he pointed at the wheelbarrow and then towards the farmhouse. The car is gone. The Farmer has gone on holiday, Bitzer whuffed. Shaun would be much more comfy in the Farmer's bed, and the Farmer would never know.

Nodding eagerly, Shaun sat up straight. A real bed! With the Farmer's teddy, and proper pillows, and soft blankets and ... and ... a television, and a DVD player, and a bathroom with a plastic shower cap and rubber ducks... His prank was working better than he could ever have imagined. Realizing he was grinning from ear to ear, he quickly flopped back, groaning.

Two minutes later, dressed in a clean pair of the Farmer's pyjamas and hugging his teddy, Shaun settled into bed with a sigh of happiness. The pillows were softer than marshmallows. Bitzer carried in the television and set it up at the end of the bed while Shaun looked through a selection of DVDs, trying to choose between a fast-paced action movie called *Blazing Tractors 6: Fields of Fury* and a documentary about sheds.

It was an easy choice. Shaun settled back with the remote control in one hoof and watched as a handsome farmer, sucking on a blade of grass, drove a tractor through fields of flame to rescue a trapped sheep. Bitzer, meanwhile, wheeled in a trolley loaded with drinks, sandwiches, cake and ice cream. Then he closed the curtains and switched off the light before tiptoeing away.

Glued to the screen, Shaun ate until his stomach groaned. Soon, cake and ice cream were smeared across the bedcovers. As the credits rolled, he picked up a cheese-and-pickle sandwich and used it to mop up some spilled lemonade, then tucked the sandwich under the pillow for later. With a happy sigh, he snuggled deeper.

This was the best prank ever. With the Farmer on holiday, days of comfort rolled out ahead of him. He yawned. When Bitzer returned from his chores, Shaun would send him to the shops for a copy of *Blazing Tractors 7: Apocalypse Plough*. In the meantime, the bed was soft and he was full of food. As the credits finished, the screen went black. The bedroom was plunged into darkness. Yawning again, Shaun felt his eyelids droop...

Shaun dreamed.

In his dream, Bitzer came into the room, grumbling about appointments that didn't exist and arguments with the dentist. Bitzer kicked his shoes off. For a moment, Shaun thought he might be awake, but then he remembered that Bitzer didn't wear shoes, or mumble about teeth. *Dreams could be crazy,* he told himself as he drifted off into sleep again. The bed springs squeaked. A weight on the bed made Shaun roll over. He reached

out and snuggled the Farmer's teddy. In his dream, it was bigger than he remembered, and extra cuddly. With a bleat of happiness, he pulled it closer, slobbering into its ear.

The teddy shrieked.

Shaun bleated crossly. With one hoof, he grabbed a pillow and whacked the noisy teddy with it. That would calm it down.

The teddy yelled, angrily.

Somewhere deep in Shaun's sleepy mind, a thought flickered. Teddies didn't shout, did they? They especially didn't shout things like, "GaahhffumminARRGH-EEEEP!"

He opened his eyes just as the lights switched on.

For a second, Shaun sat blinking in bed, surrounded by DVD boxes and crumbs and smears of cake icing. He must be still asleep, he told himself, because on the other side of the room – standing by the door with a murderous look on his face – was the Farmer.

But the Farmer was on holiday, wasn't he? Certain that he was still dreaming, Shaun stared. The Farmer's glasses were askew, and they had half a cheese-and-pickle sandwich caught in them. Shaun grinned to himself. It was a *very* strange dream. *It must have been the cheese,* he thought. Cheese always gave him odd dreams.

The Farmer stared back, his face becoming redder and redder and then going a vivid shade of purple. Shaun watched with interest and helped himself to another slice of cake.

The explosion was ... well ... *explosive*.

In the farmyard outside, Bitzer winced as the bedroom curtains blew out on a roar of "HragerrooooyaaaaarrrrrGH!" Cake and sandwiches followed, together with frightened bleats and the sounds of an alarm clock hitting the wall and pictures smashing. Less than a second later, Shaun shot out of the kitchen door, still wearing stripy pyjamas and trailing bandages as he ran, bleating, down the road. The Farmer followed in hot pursuit.

Heads appeared over the wall as the animals of Mossy Bottom Farm stopped

whatever they were doing to stare open-
mouthed. Humming to himself, Bitzer leaned
on the gate and watched Shaun disappear over
the hill with the Farmer three steps behind.
He smiled, brightly. *Shaun's leg was looking a lot
better*, he told himself. All it had needed all
along was some healthy exercise, like a nice
long run.

CHAPTER TEN:

THE LAST LAUGH

Stars twinkled down on Mossy Bottom Farm as Bitzer ticked the last chicken off his checklist and wandered back towards his kennel. By the meadow gate, he heard a whispered bleat. He stopped, and Shaun's head emerged from behind a bush. Was it safe?

Tucking his clipboard under one arm, Bitzer glanced up at the Farmer's bedroom window. Silhouetted against the curtains, the

Farmer pushed a vacuum cleaner round the room. With a whuff, Bitzer nodded at Shaun. The coast was clear.

Looking sheepish, Shaun shuffled over, his hooves behind his back and his head hung. He gave Bitzer a low bleat of apology and tried a grin. Were they still friends?

Bitzer frowned, then whuffed seriously. The pranks would have to stop. Forever. He never wanted to see another prank again.

Shuffling from hoof to hoof, Shaun nodded eagerly. The pranks had gone too far. He would never prank Bitzer again.

Bitzer held out a paw. If the pranks stopped, they could still be friends.

Shaun shook the sheepdog by the paw and bleated happily. With a sweet smile, he pointed to a large flower he was wearing on his chest. Would Bitzer like a sniff?

Bitzer's eyes widened. It was a large and exotic-looking bloom. He had never seen anything like it before. Leaning over, he took a long sniff...

Squeezing a rubber bulb hidden in his fleece, Shaun gave the gullible sheepdog a face full of water. And for the second time that day, Shaun ran for it.

This time, he was laughing.

ACTIVITIES

TOP PRANKS

1. SICKENING SPOONFUL

Carefully clean out a mayonnaise jar once it has been used up. Put some vanilla pudding or yoghurt into the jar instead. Then make sure someone is watching when you proceed to spoon it up and eat it. Gross!

2. BIG FOOT

Stuff wads of toilet paper into someone else's shoes. When they go to put them on, watch as they wonder whether the shoes have shrunk, or whether their feet have grown!

3. HUNGRY LOOKS

Get a pack of googly eyes from a craft store. Apply those little eyes to everything in the refrigerator, so the next time someone opens the door to look for a snack, they'll find a crowd looking right back!

4. A SOLID BREAKFAST

Prepare a bowl* of cereal with milk, then freeze it overnight. Don't forget to leave in the spoon. Then offer the bowl to someone for breakfast, and sit back to watch your victim's confusion and surprise...

*Use a plastic bowl, if possible, or one that has "freezer safe" written on the underside. Ceramic, porcelain or glass bowls might crack as the milk freezes.

YOU'VE BEEN PRANKED!

Someone has played a trick, scrambling all the letters of each word on this shopping list! Can you work out what the correct items are? Write them below.

- -

- -

- -

- -

- -

- -

- -

- -

Answers: TOILET PAPER, BROCCOLI, MILK, SHAMPOO, SWEETS, LEMONS or MELONS, TOOTHPASTE, PIZZA

Tiltoe Preap
Cloirboc
Klmi
Moopash
Tewsse
Nolmes
Tsottephao
Izpaz

HOW TO DRAW A MOUSE

This mouse has been known to cause mischief in several of the Tales from Mossy Bottom Farm books.

Learn how to draw him, so he can cause trouble all over!

STEP 1 Start with this shape.

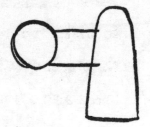

STEP 2 Add a circle and two lines. This will be his snout.

STEP 3 Now add small feet, two dots for eyes, and a smile line.

STEP 4 Draw tall loops for ears, and a rectangle for his front teeth.

STEP 5 Draw a line to make two teeth, then add whiskers, arms and a spiral for a tail. *Ta-da!*